OAK H

Bronia tells lies, particularly when she is feeling sorry for herself. When things begin to go really wrong and she and her little brother Ben are taken into Oak House for the night, in care, Bronia discovers many new and good things about herself and other people.

GATEWAY BOOKS

Belle's Bridle
Beryl Bye

The Black Pirate
James Cahill

Change With Me
Chris Savery

The Far-Farers
Chris Savery

Fisherman Jack
Mary St Helier

Friends for Joanna
Elisabeth Batt

Jamaican Schoolgirl
Elisabeth Batt

Joan's Crusade
Eileen Heming

Johnny Next Door
N.W. Hanssen

Marion's Venture
Dorothy Marsh

Nobody's Pony
Beryl Bye

Nurse Millaray
Dorothy Royce

Oak House
Susan Trought

One Too Many
Peggie C. Moody

The Open Door
Eileen Heming

Pat's New Life
Dorothy Marsh

Peter Joins In
L.V. Davidson

Pony for Sale
Beryl Bye

Ruth the Rebel
L.V. Davidson

The Secret of
Woodside Cottage
L.V. Davidson

Siege of Blackbrae
Chris Savery

Summer at End House
Diana Green

Young Elizabeth Green
Constance Savery

OAK HOUSE

SUSAN TROUGHT

LUTTERWORTH PRESS
CAMBRIDGE

To my children,
Richard, Samantha and Hannah,
with love.

Lutterworth Press
7 All Saints' Passage
Cambridge CB2 3LS

British Library Cataloguing in Publication Data

Trought, Susan
Oak house.—(Gateway)
I. Title II. Series
823'.914 [J] PZ7

ISBN 0-7188-2679-5

First published 1987 by Lutterworth Press

Typeset in Monophoto Century Schoolbook by
Vision Typesetting, Manchester
Printed in Great Britain by
The Guernsey Press Co. Ltd.,
Guernsey, Channel Islands.

CONTENTS

1

Meet Bronia

BRONIA Cole stood watching the numbers light up above the lift. She scuffed her shoes by kicking them moodily against the grey-painted rough-cast wall, and grimaced in perverse satisfaction as slight scratch marks appeared on the smooth and shiny black patent-leather.

It just was not fair! "Watch the trolley, Bronia," her mother had said as she abandoned it, along with Bronia, at the bottom of the lift which led up to the draughty car-park attached to the hypermarket.

Bronia sniffed and leant on the trolley, staring towards the bright lights of the warm shop interior.

She had not even wanted a brother in the first place. Nor a sister either, come to that. She had been quite happy as an only child for eight whole years before *he* came along and spoilt everything. And now, simply because he screamed and screeched – absolutely disgusting behaviour for a three-year-old! – her mother had left her in sole charge of the entire week's shopping while she dragged him back into the shop to buy some sweets.

She could still just see them, Ben dragging her mother along towards the checkouts where they always put the sweets, well in the way of temptation for toddlers.

"Little brat! I hate him!" she scowled in a fierce whisper, and determinedly turned her back on them.

"What was that, dear?" asked an old lady standing near, Bronia's only companion by the lift gates. "You must speak up. My hearing-aid's on the blink."

Bronia looked up and smiled her sweet little-girl smile. She knew it always screwed up the old ladies. This one, she could see, was going to be no exception.

"It's ... er ... nothing ..." she said, letting her shoulders sag and a long sigh escape her lips. She had been practising the catch in her voice all week and now she was almost sure she had got it right. She could almost feel the stirrings of sympathy in the air next to her.

The old lady came nearer.

"Ha! See . . . they can't resist the old sob stuff . . ." thought Bronia triumphantly as she watched her out of the corner of her eye. "Silly old bat!" She sniffed again, more loudly this time to make sure the hearing-aid picked it up, and let her head fall forward so that her long dark hair fell in a curtain, shading her face.

"Are you all right, dear?" enquired the old lady, bending down to peer anxiously into Bronia's face.

"Here goes ..." she thought and squeezed her eyes tightly shut to make them water. She opened them again and blinked, smiling bravely.

"Are you lost?" the old lady tried again. Bronia shook her head and gulped. She had long since perfected the shuddering gulp.

"I've only been left for a minute," she whispered and the old lady leaned nearer. "The whisper always gets 'em," thought Bronia.

"You'll have to speak up, dear," repeated the old lady, pointing to her orange-flesh-pink hearing-aid, almost obscured by the green felt hat which was well pulled down on her head.

"I'm sorry," sniffed Bronia. She suddenly threw her hair back in a dark brown cascade and squared her shoulders.

"It's the brave look now," she decided. "Always knocks 'em dead!"

"That's better," said the old lady brightly. "Things can't be that bad." She smiled kindly and put out her hand to pat Bronia gently on the shoulder with a brief bird-like movement. Bronia sensed rather than felt it through her thick jumper.

Bronia did her famous lip tremble. It had been known to make grown men go pale.

"Now come on," said the old woman. "What's it all about?"

Bronia wondered which routine to go into today. Old ladies often fell for the abandoned orphan bit, so she thought she would try that.

"My dad's dead," she began and glanced up, adding for good measure, "... and my mum. In a car crash ... last week!"

"Oh, my dear, I'm so sorry!" exclaimed the old lady, turning up her hearing-aid quickly so that she did not miss anything.

Bronia sniffed a few more loud brave sniffs and wiped away the tear which had eventually managed to trickle down her cheek.

"He was an airline pilot ..." she began, knowing from experience that if she told the truth and said he was a foreman at the local plastics factory, she would not get half as much sympathy.

The old lady nodded gravely and waited for her to carry on.

"I've been sent to live with an aunt," she continued, sighing. "But she hates me!"

"Oh, I'm sure she doesn't!" protested her new companion, fluttering her thin hands to her wrinkled throat in horror.

Bronia nodded slowly and licked her lips, warming to her theme. "Yes, she does," she insisted. "She only took me in because she wants to get her hands on my inheritance."

"But ..." began her new friend.

"She needs it for her mentally-retarded son," claimed Bronia extravagantly. "He's totally subnormal and needs twenty-four-hour care . . . that's . . . she's . . . er . . . no time for me . . ."

They stood in silence for a moment. Bronia wondered whether she had gone just a little too far this time and bit her lip. She sniffed again and lowered her eyes. Suddenly, as if coming to a great decision, the old lady rummaged in her sparsely-filled trolley and brought out a large box of milk chocolates.

"Here you are, my dear," she said, smiling kindly. "You have these. I meant to put them away for my niece for Christmas.... You know, if I buy a bit each week then my pension seems to stretch a bit further ... but you have them!" She held them out, her hands shaking slightly.

"Oh no, I couldn't!" gasped Bronia, sensing that victory was within her grasp.

"Yes, yes ... I insist.... Take them."

"But Aunty Madge would take them off me and give them to *him* – Benjamin!"

"Oh ... er ..." faltered the old lady.

"But," said Bronia quickly, wondering if she had protested just a little too much, "... if I hide them, then she'll never know, will she?" and she shot her benefactor a dazzling smile.

"That's the spirit!" beamed the old lady, and pushed the pound box of chocolates into Bronia's hands.

"Here's the lift," said the old lady. "Are you taking the trolley up?"

Bronia shook her head and glanced back into the shop again. "Aunty Madge told me to wait for her. She's gone back into the shop for her bottle of gin. . . . She'll hit me if I go away."

"Drinks as well, does she?" sighed the old lady, shaking her head. "Well, goodbye, dear, and chin up! I can see you're a brave little girl. You'll win through," she said and stepped into the lift.

"Thank you . . . thank you very much . . ." stammered Bronia and bit her lip, another gesture she had long since perfected in front of the bedroom mirror. She clutched her prize in both hands.

The lift doors closed and her face split into a wide grin. "That was not a bad effort at all . . ." she whispered to herself, turning the box of milk chocolates over to look at the price.

Then she caught a glimpse of Benjamin's red jumper as he ran along in front of their mother.

"Look! Look!" he shouted. "Bronia! Look! Sweeties! . . . You have some too . . ." and he opened his hand to offer her one from the gooey mass, his bright little face shining as he stared up at her, his big sister.

Bronia raised her eyes to heaven and gritted her teeth. Why did he always have to mangle them up in his hot little hand? They were all revoltingly sticky.

"No, thank you," she said haughtily, turning away from him.

"He was very kind to offer you one, Bronia," said her mother, walking up briskly. "Say 'thank you' to him and then he'll know he's been a good boy."

"Thank you," said Bronia shortly, closing her mouth in a thin straight line.

"What have you got there?" asked her mother, pointing to the box of chocolates.

"Sweeties!" yelled Benjamin, and Bronia held the box high up so that they were out of his reach.

"Oh," she said airily. "An old lady gave them to me because she said I reminded her of her granddaughter who was murdered a few months ago."

"That was very kind of her," murmured her mother absently, not really paying any attention as Bronia had anticipated. The lift doors slid open again and she struggled to get the trolley in. "Come on," she said over her shoulder. "Let's go and get the dinner on before Dad gets home."

Bronia smiled an inward triumphant smile as she squeezed into the small space beside her mother.

2

Bad News

THEIR battered old van rattled down the road and Bronia cringed as she always did. She felt sure that everyone was looking at them and laughing. She slid well down in the seat, and shuddered as she remembered the time when the exhaust pipe had nearly fallen off and her mother had insisted on driving the van all the way home from town with it clanging and sparking as it scraped along the road underneath them. Bronia had pointed out all the garages on the way but her mother had ignored them, saying, "They cost a fortune! Your dad will be able to fix it just as soon as he gets home from work tonight." She grimaced at the memory.

And that was another thing. Bronia hated it when her father showed her up by donning his filthy, greasy, ancient overalls and spent whole weekends lying on his back underneath the van on the short driveway.

She just knew that all their neighbours were watching from behind their lace curtains and sniggering and making snide comments. She refused to go out of the front door at such times and either stayed in her room or crept out of the back door and ran until she was far away.

Now, as they turned into the narrow street, Ben recognised where he was and began to bounce about in the back excitedly.

"Stop it!" shouted Bronia, twisting round in her seat. "Sit still – you'll break the eggs and biscuits!"

"I want a biscuit," decided Ben.

"Wait until after you've had tea," soothed Mrs Cole, glancing in the rear-view mirror to inspect the damage done by her lively three-year-old.

"I want one now," insisted Ben, and Bronia gritted her teeth to wait for the expected confrontation.

"After tea." How her mother could keep so calm Bronia just did not know. She felt that she could cheerfully strangle him at times.

Ben began to pick up the colourful packets in the large cardboard box and inspect them hopefully.

"No, Ben," said her mother again, still with only a slight edge to her voice. But it was enough. Benjamin knew when he was beaten and put the packets back none too carefully.

Bronia groaned and shot him a look of pure malice.

"It's all right," said her mother. "He's put them back now."

"He threw them in!" exploded Bronia. "They'll be all broken!"

Mrs Cole did not reply, concentrating on squeezing the van into the drive where they rattled to a halt.

Ben immediately clambered over their mother, putting sticky hands and hard-soled sandals all over her. She planted a warm kiss on his cheek as she opened the driver's door to let him out. He ran to the little blue trike which was his pride and joy and began to ride madly round the tiny lawn. Bronia watched him in despair, but it seemed to her that she was the only one who noticed that the poor lawn was almost threadbare. She sighed.

"Come on, then, Bronia," said her mother. "Help me get this lot into the house. Your dad'll be home soon."

The doorbell chimed. Bronia ignored it as she sat in front of the television set. Ben ran to the window and peered out.

"It's a man!" he declared and climbed on to the window-sill.

"Get off!" shouted Bronia.

The doorbell sounded again.

"See who it is, will you, Bronia, please?" called her mother from the kitchen. "I can't leave this chip pan."

Bronia groaned and banged her fist on the carpet. She screwed up her face, stuck her tongue out towards the kitchen, and then said brightly, "Yes, Mummy!"

She slowly backed out of the room, her eyes glued to the television screen.

The doorbell chimed once more. Bronia reluctantly tore herself away from the cartoon and went into the narrow hall. A bulky silhouette was framed in the glass panel of the doorway.

Bronia pulled the door open and stared rudely at the visitor, a large man in a navy-blue donkey jacket.

"Hello, love," he said. "Is your mum in?"

Bronia shook her head.

"Oh dear," said the man, twisting his cap in his hands. "I really wanted a word with her."

"She's gone to visit her sister in Birmingham because she's broken her leg." Bronia lied easily without thinking.

"Oh dear, oh dear," repeated the man, looking more and more worried. "I suppose you're waiting for your dad?"

Bronia nodded. Ben ran up and caught hold of her skirt. She wrenched it out of his grasp and he leant on the open door with a grubby finger stuck firmly in his mouth, staring wide-eyed at the visitor.

The man looked distractedly from one to the other and shuffled his feet.

He cleared his throat two or three times and then said, "I ... er ... I've come from the factory ..."

Bronia watched him in silence.

"Um ..." The poor man was at a loss for words. Bronia felt the familiar warm feeling of power in the pit of her stomach as she watched him squirm. She folded her arms and waited.

"I ... er ... I'll be off then," he muttered in a sudden rush and blundered away down the path. He bumped into the khaki-coloured van and dropped his cap before pedalling furiously down the road on the antique bicycle he had left propped up on their wall.

Bronia watched him go, a broad malicious smile on her face.

"Who was it?" called her mother, still busy preparing the evening meal in the kitchen.

"Just someone collecting for the children's home!" Bronia shouted back, closing the door. "I gave them 20p out of my pocket-money!"

"How kind!" said her mother, but Bronia did not hear. She was back in front of the television set.

An hour later they were still all waiting for Bronia's father to arrive home from work.

"Can't we have ours, Mum?" asked Bronia. "I'm starving!" She wandered round the tiny kitchen and sat down at the table hopefully.

"Me too!" squealed Benjamin.

"Yes, I suppose you'd better," agreed their mother. "I'll put yours on the table and go down the road to the phone box.... I'm sure I don't know where he's got to ... but perhaps he's got some overtime ..."

She hurriedly took their plates out of the

oven and put them on the table-mats. "Be careful, Ben, they're hot," she warned automatically.

Bronia sat at the table and wondered angrily why they were about the only people she knew who did not have a telephone. It was pathetic! Really, in this day and age absolutely *everyone* had a telephone. She had asked and asked but the reply had always been the same. "We can't afford it . . ." She clenched her hands in her lap.

"Shan't be a minute," said her mother, pulling on her coat and taking 10p out of the jar in the cupboard marked "Tea".

The door banged shut. Bronia moodily pushed her chips round her plate. "These are cold!" she complained. "*And* soggy! I hate soggy chips!"

Ben did not answer. His mouth was full and his plate was nearly empty.

"You are a little pig!" she said, watching him disgustedly. "I don't know how you can eat such a revolting mess!"

The sound of their mother in the hallway spurred Bronia into action. She got up quickly, scraped her plate into the plastic swing-top bin and set it back on the table with her knife and fork neatly placed side by side on it.

"I don't understand," said their mother, shaking her head as she came into the kitchen. "There's no overtime tonight. All I got was the office cleaner. She said that everyone had gone home."

"Come and have your tea," said Bronia brightly in her "dutiful daughter" tone. She got up from the table and put her empty plate in the sink. "It was delicious!"

"But . . ." began Ben and looked at the bin, but Bronia gave him such a fierce look that he stopped.

"Yes, I suppose he'll be home in a minute," said Mrs Cole. "It's so unlike him, though . . ." she added distractedly.

A loud knock on the door made them all jump. It echoed round the hall and somehow sounded ominous.

"Goodness!" exclaimed Mrs Cole. "Whoever can that be?"

"Daddy!" yelled Benjamin and ran into the hallway, laughing in anticipation.

"I bet he's forgotten his key," muttered Bronia as her mother padded towards the front door in her slippers.

A large policeman hurriedly removed his helmet as she opened the door.

"Oh, so you're back, then," he said.

"Pardon?"

"You *are* Mrs Cole, aren't you?"

"Yes, that's right."

"How's your sister?" he asked.

Mrs Cole was confused. "Have you got the right address?" she asked.

"It is Mrs Cole, isn't it? Mrs *Marion* Cole?"

"Yes," she replied, and then she suddenly had an awful thought. "Oh!" she cried, and her eyes opened wide in horror as she clapped a hand over her mouth. "It's John, isn't it?" she exclaimed. "What's happened to him?"

"Look, Mrs Cole," said the policeman gently. "Do you think I could come in?"

"Oh . . . yes . . . I'm sorry . . . yes, of course . . ." she stuttered and stood aside while the blue-uniformed figure squeezed past her. He stood, almost filling the narrow hall.

"You'd better come in here," she said, opening the door to the sitting-room. "Bronia! Take Ben into the kitchen a minute, will you, please!" she called.

The policeman nodded in approval and looked around the small but pleasant sitting-room. He indicated a chair. "May I?" he asked and sat down heavily, balancing his helmet on his ample knees. Mrs Cole sat down abruptly on the edge of the settee.

"What is it?" she asked hesitantly. "Has there been an accident? Is he . . ." She was going to say "dead" but could not bring herself to pronounce the word.

"No, no," said the policeman, as if reading her thoughts. "There's been an accident, though."

"Oh, my God!"

"He's all right. He's in hospital."

"Oh no!" wailed Mrs Cole. "Can I see him?"

"Yes, of course you can, Mrs Cole, but there

seems to have been some confusion. We had a message from the factory that you were away because you were visiting your sister in Birmingham or somewhere, and that the children were on their own waiting for their father to come home."

"I haven't got a sister ... I wouldn't leave Bronia and Ben on their own ..." said Mrs Cole vacantly in a small voice, her thoughts wholly with her husband.

"No, no, of course you wouldn't, Mrs Cole ..." said the policeman. "Oh well, never mind that now. I had come to take the children to the police station to look after them until we could get in touch with you at your sister's."

"I haven't got a sister," repeated Mrs Cole as if in a daze.

"I know that now," said the policeman patiently, seeing that she was very shocked. "Look, there's a policewoman in the car. Should I fetch her?"

Bronia's mother sat on the settee, staring into space and twisting her wedding ring round and round on her finger. She did not answer.

"Mrs Cole," he said again and she jumped.

"Oh, sorry."

"Mrs Cole, should I take the children to the police station while you go on to the hospital? WPC Jackson will take good care of them. You do drive, I suppose?" he asked gently. "... Or would you prefer it if we took you?"

"No, no. I'll be all right ... it'd be better if I had the van anyway. It would be easier to get to and fro ..."

"Yes, you're probably right," agreed the policeman. "Now, about the children ..."

"Would it be too much to ask you to look after them?" she asked, glad that someone was available to take care of them. "Is John really all right? What happened?"

"Yes, he'll be fine, Mrs Cole," replied the policeman. "There was an explosion ..."

"Oh no!"

"... but there's nothing to worry about. Come on, you can see for yourself."

3

At the Police Station

"IS the blue light flashing?" asked Ben excitedly.

"Yes, it is," smiled WPC Jackson, nodding her head and taking hold of his plump little hand again as they sat in the back of the squad car.

"Oh no," breathed Bronia. "Everyone will be looking through their curtains. They'll think we're criminals!"

"Of course they won't, dear," replied WPC Jackson briskly, but Bronia ground her teeth and slid down in her seat. She did not like to be involved in dramas that were not of her own making.

It had been a shock, of course, when their mother had explained to them all that she understood about their father's accident, but since the initial shock Bronia had steadfastly refused to think about it. She was very good at thinking only those thoughts which were pleasant to her. She gave only the briefest of backward glances at her mother as she drove off at high speed and rattled down the road. It was all just too bad! Events were happening too quickly for her to gather her wits about her. She seethed quietly to herself.

At the police station all was quiet when they arrived. The desk sergeant looked up from his newspaper and straightened up when the two children were ushered in by the policewoman.

"Hello," he said, coming towards the counter and closing the heavy black ledger, carefully putting the top back on the pen which was lying beside it. He seemed to do everything in slow motion, all his actions were calm and deliberate.

"Would you like a nice cup of tea?" he asked.

Bronia shuddered inwardly at what she thought was false concern, because she always judged people by how she herself acted.

Sergeant MacCorquindale came round the counter and picked up Ben deftly, holding him aloft easily. "You're a big boy, aren't you?" he smiled kindly. "What's your name?"

Ben stared at him wide-eyed, but did not answer.

"Here," said the sergeant, still smiling. "Would you like to try on my helmet?"

Ben's eyes grew even larger and he stuck his finger in his mouth and nodded gravely.

"Come on, then!" The dome-shaped helmet slipped right down over Ben's face and WPC Jackson pushed it backwards so that it only just balanced precariously on the back of his head. He laughed delightedly, grabbing hold of it to prevent it from falling.

Bronia regarded the scene with contempt. She felt sure that they should not have treated her as a child. She could easily have gone to the hospital with her mother, or even gone to stay with their next-door neighbours, much as she disliked them. She could have stayed at home, for that matter.

Even though she had protested at the time, her mother had over-ridden all her arguments, insisting that she should go to look after Ben so that he would not be frightened.

She looked at him, the centre of attention again, and folded her arms.

"I'm sure your father will be all right," said WPC Jackson, misreading Bronia's thoughts and silence.

"Of course he will," agreed the sergeant, regarding the strangely quiet young girl over her brother's fair head.

"Why can't I go to the hospital?" asked Bronia shortly.

The sergeant glanced at the policewoman and a slight frown puckered his forehead.

"Come on," said WPC Jackson, putting an arm lightly across Bronia's shoulders. "You'll feel better when you've had a cup of tea. Your mum will be back soon."

Bronia shrugged off the arm and stood her ground firmly. Ben wriggled round in the sergeant's arms to watch his sister solemnly.

"I want to go to the hospital," she repeated, refolding her arms.

The policewoman sighed and said patiently, "I'm sorry, my dear, but we all – your mother and father as well – think that it would be better if you stayed here until things have been sorted out. You heard what your mother said."

"What things?"

"Well, when there's been a bad accident and someone has been injured, they have to do all kinds of tests . . . X-rays and things . . . to see what needs to be done to make them better," she explained.

Bronia sniffed. It was impossible! This stupid policewoman did not understand the slightest thing! Fancy treating her like a baby . . . like Benjamin!

She looked across at her little brother. He was having a wonderful time, of course. The sergeant had sat him down on the large desk and was tickling him. Ben's squeals of laughter rang round the cream-painted room. Bronia watched him in disgust.

"He will be all right, you know," repeated the policewoman. Bronia ignored her, walked slowly and deliberately over to the hard wooden bench near the wall and sat down stiffly, her back straight as a ramrod and her hands clasped tightly in her lap.

She stared directly ahead. She was furious!

Never before had she been made to do something so much against her will. Usually she had managed to twist things, or tell tales or otherwise organise it so that everyone, both children and adults alike, did as she wanted.

This time she had been caught completely unawares and she found herself totally unprepared.

Bronia did not even consider the fact that some of the mess might have been of her own making because she had wanted to get back to her television programme and so had sent away the man from her father's factory.

She leaned her head back on to the wall. If she was furious with anyone she was furious with herself and her anger served also conveniently to push all thought of her father further into the back of her mind. She realised almost immediately that she had taken the wrong line with the policewoman, and she also knew that it was too late to try a different approach. Or was it? She regarded the two police officers at the counter from under her long dark eyelashes. Suddenly she gave a sigh, dropped her head and let her shoulders droop.

At the desk the sergeant nodded towards the solitary and obviously miserable figure and WPC Jackson walked over to sit beside her. She put her arm round Bronia again and this time the girl did not resist, but seemed to collapse towards the dark-blue uniform with a sob.

The policewoman held her tightly and let her cry until she sat up bravely and wiped her eyes – taking great care not to dry her tears completely.

"That's right," said WPC Jackson softly. "You get it out of your system. It's much better to have a good cry if you feel like it."

Bronia peeped upwards through her wet eyelashes and could see the sympathetic smile on the policewoman's face. She knew then that she could soon wrap her round her little finger. She smiled a watery smile, using her famous lip-tremble technique.

WPC Jackson nodded and patted her knee.

As they sat there the telephone rang. Sergeant MacCorquindale picked up the receiver and listened for a moment.

He frowned and glanced over to Bronia and WPC Jackson, to whom he beckoned. She leant over the desk with her back to Bronia and they had a whispered conversation. Bronia clamped her lips together in annoyance. They were obviously talking about her. She thought that they were most rude . . . and just as she was getting on so well too!

She got off the hard wooden bench where she had been pretending to read a newspaper. At first WPC Jackson had brought her some comics and some girls' magazines but these she had rejected immediately and chosen a paper.

Ben had happily dived into the dog-eared pile and begun to colour and scribble on the play pages with some colouring pencils which the sergeant had found in his drawer.

Bronia strode over to the counter and coughed loudly.

The sergeant peered over WPC Jackson's shoulder and cleared his throat. The policewoman turned round.

"Well, my dear," she began. "We have some news from the hospital."

"Can I go home now?" asked Bronia, interrupting her. WPC Jackson blinked.

"I'm afraid not," said Sergeant MacCorquindale, sitting down slowly in his chair. "You see, your father has been very badly injured and your mother must stay with him at least for tonight."

"Well, I'm not sleeping in a cell," sniffed Bronia.

WPC Jackson laughed and it was a surprisingly high, girlish sound. "I should think not!" she said. "I'll make a few phone calls and we can see what we can do." She walked quickly through a dark-green painted door and closed it behind her firmly.

Bronia stalked back to her seat, fuming. They were still treating her like a child! She was rejecting any news about her father although she did not realise it.

Ben was still happily playing with the colouring pencils. Bronia frowned and tossed her hair.

4

The Hospital

AT the hospital all was not well with Mr Cole. He had been taken into intensive care and Bronia's mother nearly fainted when she saw all the complicated equipment and wires which surrounded her husband's bed.

She whimpered and put her hand up to her mouth, her eyes filling with tears. Even though the doctor had warned her in the office before she had been allowed to see him, it still came as a great shock to see him lying there, still and pale.

"It's nothing to worry about, Mrs Cole," said the large motherly-looking nurse. "It all looks a lot worse than it really is."

"I hope so," whispered Mrs Cole.

"All this is only monitoring equipment," explained the nurse. "These machines mean we can keep an eye on him and check to see how he's doing. She stared at the screens of one or two grey metal machines for a moment and turned round smiling. "He's doing fine," she announced.

Bronia's mother pulled up a chair and sat down next to the bed. It was much higher than a normal bed and the sheets were pulled tightly round her husband's stomach. Wires and electrodes were attached to his chest with sticking plaster and ran to various machines which clicked and whirred incessantly.

John Cole lay motionless, his eyes closed. A tube ran from up his nose to behind his pillow. His normally ruddy cheeks were pale and the skin seemed tight, stretched across his wide cheekbones. Marion Cole could see dark purple shadows under his eyes.

She took hold of his hand. It felt cool and lifeless.

"Press the bell if you need anything," said the nurse. "I'll bring you a cup of tea later."

As the nurse closed the door softly behind her, a silence seemed to fall over the room, which only made the regular rhythms of the machines seem louder. Marion Cole closed her eyes, letting the noise wash over her. It was strangely comforting, even though it did look frightening at first. She sighed, feeling the beginning of a headache starting behind her eyes.

Although the kind policewoman had assured her that they would take care of them, it was only now in the quietness that she began to think about her children. She wondered where Ben and Bronia were. She suddenly realised that she was trembling, although it was not cold.

The door opened and the nurse brought in a cup of steaming hot tea.

"Here," she said. "Drink this. It'll do you good."

"Thanks."

"Do you want me to sit with you?" asked the nurse.

"Would you?"

The nurse nodded and padded round the room, checking on all the dials and screens. For such a big person she moved very gracefully.

She turned round and smiled. "He's doing fine," she repeated.

"What about Bronia and Ben?"

"Your children?"

"Yes, the policewoman said she'd look after them ..."

"And I'm sure she will," smiled the nurse.

"But ..." began Mrs Cole, and the nurse could see that she was worried and would not settle down until she knew what was happening to her children.

"Do you want me to find out what's happening to them?" she asked, understanding the dilemma immediately.

"You are kind ..." said Mrs Cole. "I ... I ... don't know what to do for the best ..." She looked over to her husband. "I know John doesn't know that I'm here but ..."

"Well, the first thing is not to worry, my dear," said the nurse kindly. "You can see that your husband is in very good hands here and I'm sure that your children are all right. But ... to put your mind at rest I'll go and phone the police station to find out exactly what's happening."

"You really are kind," repeated Mrs Cole, blowing her nose into a damp tissue she had pulled out of her coat pocket. "Aren't I being silly?"

"No, of course you're not! You've had a great shock and I do understand. You want to stay here with your husband but you also want to be with your children to look after them."

Marion Cole nodded.

"It's a problem we often have in here," smiled the nurse. "But it's nothing serious. We'll soon get it sorted out."

Bronia's mother knew that the children were all right really, but she was still worried that they might be upset and she would not be there to comfort them. She had never left them before, not even with a neighbour while she went to the shops.

At the same time she knew that she had to stay at her husband's bedside in case he regained consciousness. She was almost torn in two.

The nurse bustled out of the door again and she stood up to take off her coat. They had said she could have a bed in a nearby room, but she preferred to sit next to her husband's bed.

The chair was fairly comfortable and she settled down for a long night.

5

Oak House

BRONIA was annoyed with herself. She had almost fallen asleep. They were speeding along the deserted roads in the police car, going to the "kind lady" who would look after them until the morning. Bronia shuddered at the sugary tones of WPC Jackson as she told them about the children's home. Of course she had not exactly *said* that it was a children's home, but Bronia knew that it was.

Ben did not care. He was fast asleep, snuggled up in the blanket that WPC Jackson had wrapped round him. Bronia, although she was so tired, was still feeling angry. How dare they treat her like this! She was used to having at least some say in what happened to her. She wished her mother was there.

"Nearly there," smiled WPC Jackson, looking in her rear-view mirror. "Won't be long now."

Bronia sniffed and folded her arms, hugging herself with her hands tucked firmly up under her armpits. She stared out of the window and wished she could go home.

Their breath was steaming up the window so

she slowly and carefully rubbed a small hole so that she could see outside.

They were not in a part of the town that she knew. The short, brightly lit streets with illuminated shop signs had suddenly given way to long, sweeping avenues of large Victorian houses sitting smugly on either side.

This had obviously once been a very prosperous part of the town. Now most of the dwellings had been made into small private hotels or plush insurance offices. Bronia caught tantalising glimpses of them in the darkness, standing well back from the road. She wondered about the people who had had them built originally and imagined horse-drawn carriages and servant girls giggling when the coachmen whistled at them.

"Mrs Bailey said she would look out for us," said WPC Jackson over her shoulder, interrupting Bronia's thoughts. "She often helps us out at a time like this."

Bronia glared doggedly out of the window, her little porthole now becoming misty again. Angrily she tossed her head as she felt hot tears – real ones for a change – pricking at the back of her eyelids and threatening to overflow and run down her cheeks. Why had their mother left them? Could it be, she wondered, because she preferred their father; because she did not like her children? Was it because, Bronia gulped, because she told so many stories? Were they lies? She had never thought of them like that before.

A cold knot clenched in her stomach, and she pushed the thought away before it had time to take hold of her.

She looked over at Ben. He was still peacefully asleep, his fair head resting comfortably on the back of the seat. Bronia felt a sudden and totally unexpected rush of affection for her little brother. This was definitely something that had never happened before.

She put her hand out to touch his blond hair, but withdrew it sharply without knowing why. She was confused. She glanced up and saw WPC Jackson watching her in the rear-view mirror. She pushed her hands deeply into her pockets and stared at her feet in the darkness in the back of the car. She wished again for the umpteenth time that everything could be as it had been when she had woken up that morning. Without thinking, she began to mutter a fervent prayer. "Please, God. Let it be back to yesterday again . . ." but she knew it was a silly thing to pray for even though it made her feel better.

Gravel crunched under the wheels and the large car pulled up smoothly to a graceful stop.

"Here we are!" announced WPC Jackson unnecessarily.

Bronia secretly brushed away the tears with the back of her hand and got out on to the drive. A massive dark house stood before her and, as she watched, the front door opened to spill warm light on to the stone steps which led down to the lawn and gravel driveway. Bronia peered about her in the gloom. The solid square house was like something she had only ever read about in books or seen in films. She gazed at it and was almost overwhelmed by the sheer size of the building. She felt very small and alone.

A little dumpy figure stood silhouetted in the doorway and WPC Jackson waved.

"You go on, dear," she said to Bronia. "Mrs Bailey's expecting you. I'll bring Ben."

Bronia took a small step forward and stopped. A sudden gust of wind disturbed the branches of a huge oak tree which shaded the lawn. She shivered and had a sudden picture in her mind of her father laughing. She shut her eyes and tossed her head to get rid of it.

"Come along, dear!" called Mrs Bailey, beckoning her vigorously from the tall arched doorway. "You'll catch cold if you stay out there!"

Bronia turned to watch WPC Jackson struggling to get Ben out of the back of the car without disturbing him. She knew that she would usually be pleased to watch someone struggling, especially someone who had so far got the better of her, but this time she just watched passively and thought that her mother never had such difficulty in handling her younger child. She had never thought of it before, nor compared her mother so favourably in this way.

She walked slowly up the path, trying to decide which plan of action would bring her the most sympathy. She decided that the "brave little soldier" routine was called for, so she straightened her shoulders slightly and pushed her hair away from her face in a way she knew was guaranteed to win a bravery award.

Mrs Bailey bustled down the cold stone steps with her arms outstretched. Bronia stopped a few feet away from her and stood stiffly, looking at her with her bottom lip clenched tightly in her teeth.

"Hello, Bridget," said Mrs Bailey in a soft Irish brogue.

"Bronia."

"Bronia, is it? Well, that's a rare name for a lovely young lass like yourself and no mistake."

Bronia shrugged and suddenly had an idea. "My family is not English," she said, and managed to put a slight foreign accent into her voice.

"Oh really? Is that so? And to be sure neither is mine ..." smiled Mrs Bailey. "Well, you come along in and you can tell me all about it. That's right now," she added as WPC Jackson stepped past her with the sleeping Ben in her arms.

"Put him in the little room," she said. "Poor little darling must be worn out."

Bronia followed her up the steps and was quite grateful when the heavy wooden door thumped shut behind her and shut out the cold chill of the huge garden outside.

"All the other children are in bed," announced Mrs Bailey.

"Oh!" Bronia was startled. She had not realised that other children would be there. Her heart sank. It really was a children's home then. They really did exist. They were not just something you read about in story books.

The daydream she had had in the police station about being abandoned in a children's home did not now seem to be so romantic in reality. She felt quite deserted.

"It's very late, you know," said Mrs Bailey. "It should have been lights out at nine o'clock for older ones like you."

"Nine o'clock?" echoed Bronia.

"It's more than late enough," continued the soft voice. "Especially when you may have to go to school the next morning."

Bronia sighed. It was worse than she had imagined, but then she brightened when she realised how she could use all this to gain attention when she went back home. She smiled to herself and felt the familiar warm feeling in the pit of her stomach at the thought of all the interest she would create at school.

Strangely, the feeling went away again almost before it had begun and she was left with an empty clenched knot instead.

She dismissed the disappointment she felt and knew that she had first to get a grip on the situation. The last few hours had been very worrying because she had had no say at all in what was happening to her.

"Mrs Bailey," she began, putting the well-rehearsed catch into her voice.

"Yes, dear?"

"Will we ever go home again? . . ." she asked dramatically, lowering her eyes and letting her hair fall forward, but this time as she did so she found that she really did want to know the answer and was desperately frightened that it might not be the right one.

"Of course you will, dear," said the house-mother kindly, after a quick puzzled glance at the forlorn figure. "You come along into the kitchen now. I've made the fire up and I can soon have a mug of cocoa ready."

Bronia allowed herself to be led into the large high-ceilinged kitchen. In one corner was a huge fireplace where behind a fireguard a roaring coal fire was blazing. Bronia had never seen a real coal fire before as they had a modern teak-surrounded gas one at home. She stood staring into the leaping flames and put out her hands to warm them. It was very, very comforting.

"That's right, dear," said Mrs Bailey as she busied herself at the stove. "You sit yourself down by the fire and get warm."

WPC Jackson came back into the kitchen and took off her hat, laying it carefully on the scrubbed pine table which dominated the centre of the room.

"He's well away," she said, meaning Ben. "Little love ..."

"Sure he is ... he'll probably sleep until morning," agreed Mrs Bailey.

The warmth had made Bronia sleepy again and she felt her eyelids drooping in spite of her determination to stay awake as long as possible. She got up and stood with her back to the fire, feeling the heat seep into her clothes.

"Here you are, dear," said Mrs Bailey, handing her a mug of steaming cocoa.

"Thank you," she said, taking the proffered mug after only a slight hesitation and sitting down on the multi-coloured rug.

"Mrs Bailey's cocoa is famous round here," said WPC Jackson cheerfully, making herself comfortable in the huge saggy armchair next to the fire. "No other tastes quite like it," and she took a long appreciative drink from her own mug.

Bronia took a short sip and, in spite of her resolution that she would not like anything about this place, she found that it was indeed delicious and had soon finished it all.

"Come on, then," said Mrs Bailey, taking

the mug from Bronia's hand. "I've put you in with Sarah."

Again Bronia felt her spirits plummet. She was now being asked to share a room with someone she had never even met before! No! It was worse than that!

She was being *told* that she was sharing and she had never shared a room in her life! All this was so awful. She continued to sit sullenly by the fire, her fingers twisting the long pile of the rug.

Mrs Bailey misunderstood her actions. She smiled and said, "I know it's lovely and warm down here by the fire. We all love this room, but it is very late – it's almost midnight! – and I have put a hot-water bottle in your bed to take the chill off it."

She stood, hands on hips, in front of the silent little figure, her navy-blue bulk almost blocking out the fire.

Reluctantly Bronia got to her feet. The policewoman smiled and nodded encouragingly from the depths of her armchair. Bronia felt herself smile back slightly before she could stop herself. She followed Mrs Bailey into the hall.

Like all hallways in this type of house, it was almost a room in itself; the marble floor was chequered in black and white and a large mahogany table gleamed softly in the dim light from the landing. The fresh flower arrangement gave off a musky scent which seemed strangely exciting in the enclosed shadows.

The wide staircase creaked under their combined weight. Mrs Bailey pulled out a large bunch of keys, selected one and opened a tall cupboard on the landing.

She rummaged in it for a moment and then produced a neatly-folded nightdress patterned with teddy bears which she held out to Bronia.

"I can't wear that!" she protested in a loud voice, before she had had time to think. Her shouted words echoed round the old house and seemed to hang in the air accusingly.

"Why ever not?" asked Mrs Bailey, firmly closing and locking the cupboard door. Bronia caught the steely look in her kind brown eyes. Despite her obvious kindness, Bronia could see that the house-mother of this children's home was a force to be reckoned with.

Surprisingly, and without knowing why, Bronia vowed there and then that she would make Mrs Bailey like her. She had never wanted anyone to like her before. She usually presumed that they would not and so she used them for her own amusement. Perhaps it was that Bronia did not really like herself very much.

"I'm not used to second-hand clothes," she murmured quietly, looking at the offending article where Mrs Bailey had plonked it into her arms.

"Well, it's clean, young lady, which is more

than I can say about your hands," stated Mrs Bailey. "I'll show you where the bathroom is and you can have a good wash."

Bronia looked down at her hands and saw that the hours she had spent in the police station had made them very grimy. Her nails had disgusting black rims. Again she felt foolish. Mrs Bailey was right. There was no sense in her saying that she would not wear such an obviously clean nightgown when she must look like a tramp. She bit her lip and felt a dark-red flush bloom on her cheeks. She was not used to feeling embarrassed; she was more used to being the cause of embarrassment to others. She did not like it. She did not like it at all. It was certainly not an experience she wished to repeat. She bent her elbows and pulled the nightdress towards her chest while trying at the same time to hide her awful nails in the palms of her hands.

Mrs Bailey bustled away down the corridor without a backward glance, expecting Bronia to follow her.

Bronia decided to start again. She took a deep breath and stood her ground.

"Mrs Bailey," she whispered and squeezed her eyes so that the tears would start. The motherly figure stopped and turned round, poised with her hand about to turn a massive doorknob.

"Yes, dear?"

Bronia stood with her shoulders slumped –

the picture of misery. She sniffed loudly and found that it was not all play acting. The tears came readily and easily.

Mrs Bailey padded back down the corridor. "What is it?" she asked softly.

Bronia sniffed again and slowly lifted her tear-stained face to look up at her.

"I'm sorry . . ." she whispered. "I didn't mean anything . . . it's just . . . it's just that . . ." and she sobbed suddenly, dropping the nightdress and covering her face with her hands. This time the movements were entirely natural, not one had been planned in advance.

Mrs Bailey bent down and gathered her up into her arms and held her against her well-padded frame. Bronia found that her sobs were real and she leaned on the middle-aged Irish woman and cried as she could never remember crying before. She could not have stopped even if she had wanted to.

"There, there . . ." murmured Mrs Bailey, stroking her dark hair. "Everything will be all right. You have a good weep now, girl. It's a terrible thing to have happened to your family, but you'll be all right here until your mam comes to fetch you. I'll say a special prayer for you before I go to bed tonight . . .'

Bronia's shuddering sobs slowly quietened down a little and she pulled away from the embrace. She was amazed at herself but surprisingly felt a good deal less hurt and lost and wretched than she had done when she arrived.

She sniffed and wiped her eyes with her knuckles in an oddly childish gesture, leaving dark-grey streaks on her cheeks.

"There now," smiled Mrs Bailey. "You'll feel better in the morning after you've had a good night's sleep."

Bronia nodded, not daring herself to speak. She was not used to her true feelings being so strong that she could not control them. She felt very mixed-up.

6

A Worrying Night

THE nurse shook her shoulder gently. "Wake up, Mrs Cole," she said. Bronia's mother groaned and stretched herself. In spite of the fact that she had been so worried, she had fallen into a deep if rather troubled sleep on the chair while still holding her husband's hand. She yawned and then looked about her, startled and not remembering for a moment where she was.

"It's six o'clock," said the nurse. "And we want to do a few more tests, so I've brought you a cup of tea and when you've drunk it I'll show where you can have a wash and freshen yourself up."

Gratefully she took the cup and drank deeply. The heating in the room had made her mouth very dry. She looked over at her husband. He had not moved at all during the night. The machines were still flickering and bleeping, but they were the only signs that he was still alive. His breathing was so shallow that she could not see his chest move.

She put out a hand and gently brushed a lock of dark hair away from his forehead. She marvelled at how like Bronia he looked. She smiled tenderly at him. They were so alike, too, although they would both deny it. Both were strong-willed and determined.

"This way," said the nurse and held the door open. With one more backward glance at her husband, Marion Cole followed the young nurse down the corridor, still clutching the empty tea cup in her hand.

"Is there a phone I could use?" she asked as she was ushered into a tiny room containing a bed and a wash-basin.

"I'll bring you the trolley," smiled the nurse, taking the cup and backing out of the room, opening the door expertly with her foot.

Mrs Cole sat down on the bed and looked round her. The cream-painted walls were plain except for one print of a seascape which hung over the bed. A mirror was screwed on to the wall above the wash-basin and she walked over to it stiffly, holding her aching back, to stare at her reflection. "What a mess," she said to herself, and brushed the unruly fringe back from her forehead. "Ugh!" She leant on the basin and sighed.

"There we are," said the nurse brightly as she trundled in the trolley with the mobile telephone. "Just dial 9 and then any number you want. It takes 10p coins."

"Thanks."

"If you need anything else just ring the bell," said the nurse, pointing to a red button next to the bed.

"Right. Thanks. I must look a mess."

"Well, you've had a long night," said the nurse with a smile. "You should have come in here and had a good night's rest."

"I know ..." sighed Mrs Cole, "But I just couldn't leave him alone in there with all those machines . . . even if he didn't know I was there."

"I understand," said the nurse. "You have a wash and brush up now. The doctor will soon be finished and you can go and sit with him again."

The door closed behind her with a soft click. Marion Cole could hear the sounds of the hospital waking up, the voices of the staff as they went off duty and the faint clattering of the tea-trolley as it was pushed from ward to ward.

She sighed and sat down on the bed again. She picked up her handbag to sort out some change for the telephone.

It seemed to ring for a long time before there was any reply.

"Hello? Can I speak to WPC Jackson, please? . . . Oh . . . she's gone off duty . . . yes . . . I'd forgotten she must be on nights . . . well, my name is Marion Cole and I believe she was kindly looking after my children for a while. . . . Oh yes . . . that's right . . . yes . . . if you could, please. . . . Thank you . . . goodbye."

Saying the number she had been given again and again under her breath, she rummaged in her bag for another 10p. This time the ringing tone had hardly begun before the receiver was picked up and a soft Irish voice said, "Oak House."

"Mrs Bailey?"

"Yes ..."

"My name is Marion Cole and I believe you've got Bronia and Ben ..."

"That's right, dear. They're fine. You're not to worry about them, now ..."

"Are you sure? ... I mean, I could come over and fetch them ..."

"No ... no, you stay where you are, dear, until you're quite sure that everything is all right.... Jenny – WPC Jackson, that is – explained it all to me last night.... And how is your husband?"

"I'm not sure ..."

"Oh dear."

"They're doing some more tests at the moment."

"Well, I'm sure he'll be all right, dear. He's in the best place, you know. It's a very good hospital."

"Yes, I know. They've ... *You've* all been very kind."

"That's all right, dear. Don't you worry about your little ones now. I'll look after them."

"Thank you, Mrs Bailey. I'll come for them as soon as I can."

"I know you will, dear."

"And ... Mrs Bailey?"

"Yes, dear?"

"Give them both my love ..."

"I will, dear. Don't worry." The receiver clicked and the dialling tone replaced the Irish brogue.

"Poor little loves . . ." Bronia's mother whispered to herself. "They'll think I've forgotten them."

A sudden knock on the door made her jump and she dropped the telephone receiver with a clatter on the trolley and then smiled at her own nervousness.

"Come in!" she called.

A young nurse popped her head round the door. "Mrs Cole?" she asked.

"Yes."

"The doctor would like a word with you."

"Oh." Mrs Cole felt her heart sink. She was sure they were going to tell her something dreadful.

"But I haven't had time to have a wash or brush my hair or anything yet," she protested, subconsciously trying to put off the evil moment. "I must look a mess . . ."

"That's OK," said the nurse. "I'll come back in a couple of minutes."

Bronia's mother splashed lukewarm water on her face hurriedly and pulled a comb through her hair. She had only just finished when the nurse came back.

The doctor's office was not far away and the young nurse left her after knocking on the door and announcing her arrival.

"Ah, Mrs Cole," beamed the white-coated

man, rubbing his hands together as he came round the desk. "I've just had a look at your husband."

Mrs Cole looked at him and wondered why all doctors and nurses smiled so much. "How is he? ..." she began.

"He's fine," smiled the doctor, pulling an easy chair into the middle of the room for her to sit on. She wished they would not all keep saying the same thing. How could he be fine if he didn't move or speak and had hundreds of machines attached to him? Did they all think she was stupid or something?

"I believe you have children ..." continued the doctor.

She nodded. "Yes, they're at Oak House at the moment."

"Ah yes ... excellent place ... splendid person, Mrs Bailey ... salt of the earth ..." The doctor seemed to speak in shorthand.

"It's not like home ..."

"No, of course not," said the doctor, letting his smile slip a bit and returning to sit behind his desk. "Now, about your husband. John, isn't it?"

Again she nodded, biting her lip. She suddenly felt light-headed.

The doctor pulled a pale-pink file towards him over the desk and opened it. He picked up the top sheet of paper and tapped it with his forefinger, studying it carefully. "He's had some sort of blow to the head, you know ..." he began slowly, as if talking to himself. "The X-rays show that he has a hairline fracture of the skull. . . ."

"Oh no! . . ." she wailed.

"That's nothing these days," explained the doctor, glancing up at her briefly. "He'll wake up soon with a bit of a headache, that's all. . . . No, the thing that really concerns us at the moment is that he has a back injury as well."

"Oh." She felt sick. She *knew* they had been keeping something from her.

"Hmmm . . ." continued the doctor, still reading his notes. "It appears from this accident report that the explosion caused him to fall from a ladder and he not only hit his head but also landed awkwardly. He may . . . just *may*, mind you . . . have damaged his spine."

"Oh no! You mean that he's broken his back?"

"We're not sure yet. The X-rays we have just taken will show us more clearly. It will be easier when he regains consciousness, of course."

"Will he be all right?" she gulped, gripping the arms of the chair so tightly that her knuckles showed white.

"We'll know more when we've studied the X-rays . . ." repeated the doctor, but his words only made Marion Cole worry more. What was it that he was trying to tell her?

A sudden thought came to her. "Are you

trying to tell me that he won't be able to walk again?" she asked, horrified.

"It may not come to that at all." The doctor smiled his professional smile. "Only time and the X-rays will tell. That is the *worst* thing that could happen. But I warn you that there is a very slight possibility that he may be paralysed."

He put his papers down and closed the file, folding his hands on the top of it and lacing his fingers together as if to underline the gravity of the situation. He looked at her over the top of his glasses.

Mrs Cole felt the room spin round uncontrollably and then blackness overwhelmed her.

She fell to the floor in a dead faint.

7

Bronia Meets the Others

EVERYTHING considered, Bronia had slept very well. The bed was comfortable and snugly warm with the hot-water bottle which Mrs Bailey had put in for her. As the early morning light began to filter through the yellow cotton curtains, she stirred and then woke up abruptly.

She sat up in bed and rubbed her eyes with her knuckles. She had not been able to see the room properly the night before because the other girl – called Sarah, Mrs Bailey had said – had been asleep, so they had had to creep about in the dark.

Now as she hugged her knees to her chest she looked about her with great interest.

It was quite a big room with a very high ceiling. There was an enormous iron fireplace on one wall, with an embroidered firescreen in front of it. There were built-in wardrobes which were obviously a new addition and someone, she presumed Sarah, had put pictures and posters of cats all over one wall. The floor had dun-coloured linoleum on it but there were brightly-coloured rugs, one next to each bed and a larger one in front of the fireplace.

The other single bed in the room was identical to the one in which she had spent the night. Even the bedspread had the same orange and yellow flower pattern on it.

Bronia twisted herself round to try to see what her room-mate looked like. All she could make out was a shock of blonde curly hair lying on the pillow. She sighed and pulled her knees up closer. Perhaps it would not be so bad if she could imagine that she was at boarding-school or something and her parents were rich and famous. She smiled slightly as she let her imagination take over. That was it ... her father was a millionaire and her mother was a world-famous ballet dancer on tour. She had been left in this exclusive Swiss finishing-school to perfect her French before being sent to St Moritz for the season ...

She glanced over at Sarah again. She could see the rhythmic rise and fall of the bedclothes as she slept.

Carefully she pulled back her own bedclothes and got out of bed to tiptoe towards the window. Her feet felt very cold on the floor. She pulled the lemon-coloured curtains slightly apart and peered outside. It was almost fully light and she could hear the slowly fading sounds of the dawn chorus. The mysterious and forbidding garden of the night before was very different in the daylight.

Through the early morning mist she could see that it was simple yet imposing in design and obviously well-tended. She wondered vaguely if there was a gardener. It was definitely too much for Mrs Bailey to do on her own.

As she looked down on to the wide sweeping lawns and dense fringe of trees, she became aware that someone was moving behind her. She turned round slowly.

Sarah had turned over and had flung her arms above her head, her fingers touching the dark wood of the headboard. She was almost awake. Bronia stood still, watching her. Sarah had a round face with a sprinkling of freckles across her small nose. As Bronia studied her, she suddenly opened her bright blue eyes and stared at her unblinking as if she had suddenly become aware that she was under some kind of scrutiny. Just as suddenly she looked away and snuggled down in the bed again, pulling the covers tightly up to her chin and yawning.

Bronia felt most disconcerted, almost as if someone had looked right inside her, as if she had bared her soul.

"You must be Bridget," murmured the figure in the bed.

"Bronia."

"Pardon?" The piercing blue eyes shot open again.

"My name is Bronia, not Bridget." Bronia lifted first one cold foot off the floor and then the other. She wriggled her toes.

"Oh – foreign," said Sarah disparagingly into her pillow and turned over to go back to sleep.

Bronia stood glaring with her mouth wide open. She had never been dismissed in such a way! She rubbed one frozen foot on the back of her leg.

"Excuse me!" she said loudly. "I'm going to the bathroom."

Her fury mounted even more when Sarah put out her arm to wave airily to her without uttering a sound.

She stamped towards the door, grabbing the towel Mrs Bailey had given to her the night before.

"Well, really!" she exclaimed as she stepped out into the corridor and slammed the door shut behind her. She had not realised that it would make such a loud noise as it boomed and echoed round the huge old house. She stood stock still, panic-stricken. Another door opened a little further down the long corridor and a small face peered out, blinking sleepily.

"Ben?" she whispered. "Ben, is that you?" and she ran towards him to hug him, as she realised that she had never been so pleased to see anyone in her whole life. She held on to his little body and he felt warm and soft. He had obviously woken up and got out of bed immediately.

"Where's Mummy?" he asked when she finally put him down.

"She's with Daddy."

"In hospital?" he lisped, his little tongue tripping over the big new word.

"Yes."

"I want Mummy ..." he said, and his lip began to tremble and his eyes filled with tears as he stared about the strange place. Bronia realised that he had never seen it before as he had been fast asleep when they had arrived the night before. He must be very frightened and bewildered.

"Mummy'll be back soon," she said softly, kneeling beside him on the rough carpet. "We'll be able to go home soon." As she spoke she understood that she was the only one that Ben knew in this place and she must look after him. It was a strange feeling, to be suddenly responsible for someone else. She frowned, not quite sure if she liked the idea.

"Come on," she said, getting up and putting an awkward but intimate arm round his shoulders. "If we wish very hard and say a prayer together to ask God to make everything all right again, then it'll feel better."

"All right," said Ben and shut his eyes tightly and put his hands together as he had been taught at playschool. He moved his lips but Bronia could not hear the words. He suddenly stopped, opened wide his bright eyes and grinned. "That's better!" he said. "Jesus said it will be all right: Mummy will come soon."

Bronia smiled down at him and ruffled his

hair. Ben held tightly on to her hand as they walked together down to the kitchen, where Bronia knew there would be a warm welcome for them.

"I want a drink," demanded Ben.

"OK. We'll have one in a minute," she promised as they slowly negotiated the stairs.

Mrs Bailey was busily washing up at the sink as they pushed open the door. As Bronia hoped, there was a large fire blazing away and Ben's eyes opened wide in amazement when he saw it. He let go of her hand and walked towards it, fascinated.

Bronia followed him protectively, self-conscious when she realised she had acted instinctively.

"You're not to go too near," she warned as he put out his hands. "You'll get burned." She moved the fireguard a little more firmly towards the grate.

"Well, hello there, young Ben," smiled Mrs Bailey, turning round from the sink and wiping her sudsy hands on her apron. "You were fast asleep when you came here last night."

Ben ignored her in the way only very young children can, still staring at the fire. Mrs Bailey smiled again, her eyes twinkling. "Would you like a drink?" she asked. He nodded, still not able to drag his eyes away from the orange flames.

"Come on, Bronia," she said. "You can help

me to make the breakfasts."

"But . . ." Bronia was about to protest that she hated cooking, but something stopped her. A tiny niggling voice in her head was insisting faintly that grown-ups did not say things like that. She looked at Ben and, deciding he would be quite safe, she walked over to the sink.

"What do you want me to do?" she asked in a small voice.

"Well, dear," said Mrs Bailey brightly, "you can begin by setting the table. There will be six of us." If she knew about the inner struggle that Bronia was having with herself she showed no sign.

She turned back to the sink and plunged her plump arms into the suds again.

"Six?"

"Yes, there's the three of us and Sarah, William and Thomas."

Mrs Bailey showed her where all the dishes and cutlery were kept and Bronia found she quite enjoyed setting out things on the huge table in the middle of that warm and friendly room.

Ben scrambled up to sit on the bench and drank his milk greedily as soon as it was put in front of him. He kept turning round to look at the fire and Bronia found she was afraid that he was going to fall off and hurt himself. No longer was her first thought that it would serve him right. She was surprised at how agreeable she found these thoughts.

"That's a good girl!" exclaimed Mrs Bailey when she had finished and Bronia glowed at the praise. "The cereals are in that cupboard over there. You choose which you want and help yourself."

"I want those!" announced Ben, pointing to a large box of cornflakes as Bronia opened the tall cupboard in the corner. It was crammed full with provisions.

"So you shall, young man," laughed Mrs Bailey. "He's certainly not off his food, is he?" she said.

"He's a little pig!" agreed Bronia, finding that she was smiling too.

Mrs Bailey wiped her hands and sat down with them at the table, helping Ben to put cornflakes in his blue striped bowl and then supervising as he poured the creamy milk on top.

They ate for a while in silence. The homely kitchen was very restful and Bronia could feel herself relaxing. Mrs Bailey's soft voice was soothing as she began to talk about Oak House.

"It used to belong to a very rich family," she began. "But they fell on hard times and had to sell it. Well, of course, it's too big for one family these days so no one wanted to buy it for a long time. Such a beautiful house it is too..." she said wistfully. "Anyway, eventually the Council decided to buy it and turn it into a home for children who needed a temporary place to stay." She told it as if it were a fairy story – well-loved and often told.

"Can I have some more?" piped up Ben, holding up his empty dish.

"Please may I . . ." Bronia corrected him automatically as she had heard her mother correct both of them on many occasions.

"Of course you can, dear. It's nice to see someone enjoy their food so much," smiled Mrs Bailey, and she poured another generous helping into his bowl.

"Do you live here then as well?" asked Bronia, really interested.

"Yes, dear. We – that is, my husband and I – have a flat at the back of the house. He works in the Council offices and I used to be a nurse. We have to sleep in, it's part of the job. We couldn't leave children alone in the house all night. I'm a very light sleeper so I can hear if there is any disturbance."

Bronia thought what a strange job it was and said, "Don't you get sick of being wakened in the middle of the night and having strange kids dumped on you?"

Mrs Bailey laughed at the directness of the question. "No, dear. It's all part of the job."

"I would," declared Bronia.

"No, you wouldn't, not if you loved all children as I do," replied Mrs Bailey, a serious expression on her face for once. "I always looked after little ones, even when I was small. I was the eldest of ten children and so I had to help my mam with all my little brothers and sisters."

"Gosh! Ten children!" said Bronia.

Mrs Bailey nodded. "There are quite a few big families in my part of Ireland," she said. "So when Charlie and I didn't have any of our own, well, I sort of missed it."

Bronia looked hard at Mrs Bailey. It seemed incredible that a woman like her should not have any children of her own.

"Morning, Aunty Bee!" called a high voice from the doorway.

"Hello, Tommy!" she smiled and got up from the table to pick up the small boy who had just wandered into the room.

"This is Thomas," she announced. "But most people call him Tommy. He's staying with us for a little while because his mammy's in hospital."

Tommy nodded solemnly and Ben echoed, "Hospital."

"Yes, Tommy," said Mrs Bailey, speaking directly to the little boy in her arms. "Ben's daddy is in hospital too and his mammy has to stay with him . . . so you'll have a playmate for a couple of days, won't you?"

The tiny figure in the green pyjamas struggled out of her grasp and clambered onto the bench. Bronia suddenly thought of Sarah upstairs and wondered why she was staying at Oak House.

Tommy settled down next to Ben and they

ate their cornflakes while watching each other seriously. Bronia felt herself smile as she watched them.

"Where's William?" asked Mrs Bailey suddenly.

"He's coming ... he's just ... er ..." faltered Tommy.

"He's not annoying Sarah again, is he?" she asked and Bronia could see the steely glint come into her eye again, this time, however, tempered with a slight amused spark.

"We ... ell ..." Tommy wriggled on his bench, not wanting to tell tales on his "best-friend-in-all-the-world". He stuck his spoon in his mouth almost as if to hold his tongue down so that he could not tell.

"He is! The little monkey! ... Isn't he?" she asked, and without waiting for a reply she quickly opened the door and shouted, "William! You leave Sarah alone now ... do you hear me?"

There was no reply from upstairs.

"William!" shouted Mrs Bailey again, in a warning tone this time, and they could vaguely hear a muffled shriek and running footsteps from the depths of the house.

Thomas looked at Bronia and smiled lop-sidedly. "William's my brother," he announced proudly, lisping through the gaps in his teeth.

"Oh," replied Bronia, secretly very pleased that this unknown brother was annoying the snooty Sarah.

"He's eleven," continued Tommy.

"I'm three," said Ben, not wanting to be left out of the conversation. "I'm big now."

"Well, you're not as big as me 'cos I'm six," said Tommy, putting his spoon down in the middle of his empty cereal bowl.

"He is quite big for three." Bronia found herself defending her little brother for the first time in her life. Tommy looked at her and then regarded Ben with more interest, as if he knew how big a three-year-old should be.

Mrs Bailey came back into the room. "Ooooh!" she said. "Just what are we going to do about that brother of yours, Tommy?"

"Sarah's naughty,' said Tommy, as if that explained everything.

"No, she isn't really, Tommy," chided Mrs Bailey. "Everyone does naughty things at one time or another."

"Not me!" grinned Ben, looking round at them all in turn and sticking his chest out.

"Oh no, not much," muttered Bronia, but she said it rather more as a statement of a well-loved family secret than as a criticism.

"I'm sure you're a very good boy," said Mrs Bailey, smiling at him.

The door opened abruptly and a thin tousle-haired boy stood grinning in green striped pyjamas which were rather too small for him, the trouser legs ending halfway up his calves.

"Hello, Aunty Bee," he said and Bronia felt herself giggle at the ill-concealed impishness in his eyes. They sparkled with mischief in his otherwise very pale face.

"Have you been annoying Sarah?" asked Mrs Bailey, frowning.

"Only a bit . . ." he grinned, agreeing cheerfully as he walked towards the fire and held out his hands.

A small smile flickered at the corner of her mouth. William's good humour certainly was most infectious. "Well, don't let me catch you!" she said. "Now, what would you like for your breakfast?"

Again the room became quiet. Ben watched William carefully and Tommy looked at them, knowing that his brother was something special. Mrs Bailey gathered up a basket of newly-washed clothes and went through the back door to put them on the line.

She was hardly out of the room before Tommy ran round the table towards his brother.

"Did you do it?" he asked eagerly and William frowned, glancing towards the open back door before he nodded, his face splitting into an enormous satisfied smile.

"Was she very cross?" asked Tommy breathlessly.

"Not half . . ." grinned William, thinking of the spider he had put on Sarah's pillow before waking her up with a wet flannel.

Ben stared at the brothers wide-eyed. He was not used to the company of big boys and he was spellbound.

"What's your name?" Tommy asked Bronia suddenly, turning towards her.

"Bronia."

"What?"

"Bronia."

"That's a queer name," said William, pouring more cornflakes and milk into his bowl.

"'Tisn't!" said Ben. "That's my sister."

"Still a queer name," insisted William.

Bronia looked at him. He was about the same age as her, but he was much smaller and seemed younger somehow. She shrugged.

"Foreign, is it?" he asked.

"Yes – it's Polish," she said, telling the absolute truth for once without embroidering it.

"You Polish then?" he asked, his mouth full of cornflakes, but still watching her intently with his bright twinkling eyes.

She shook her head without thinking. The day before she would have taken this golden opportunity to tell a wonderful tale. Today, however, she did not feel the need to, nor did the possibility of making someone believe her stories, however far-fetched, seem to be very exciting. "No, but my great-grandma was, though. It was her name," she said.

Here, in this friendly atmosphere where everyone just accepted everyone else, probably because they were all in more or less the same boat, she felt that there was no need to tell lies or invent things to make herself seem more interesting. They seemed to be interested in her anyway. She realised with astonishment that it was quite a relief.

"Cor!" said Tommy, gazing at her. "Fancy having a Polish granny!" and they all laughed, including Bronia.

Mrs Bailey came back inside, her cheeks flushed with the cold air in the garden. "You all getting to know each other then?" she smiled as she heard the laughter.

"She's got a Polish granny!" giggled Tommy, pointing to Bronia.

"Yes," said Mrs Bailey seriously, looking her straight in the eye. "She said something about that last night."

Bronia felt her stomach turn over. She remembered how she had put on a foreign accent when she had first arrived. She felt mortified.

"But ..." she began, and found that she could not look Mrs Bailey directly in the face. She had never felt this way before. She felt hot and yet shivery and cold, all at the same time.

"Hmmm!" said the house-mother, and began to clear away the breakfast dishes. If the others had noticed any tension or unspoken words in the air they did not mention it. Bronia felt sure that they must somehow sense that something was wrong, but as she glanced tentatively at first one and then the other they all seemed to be completely unaware of the complex emotions which were tearing round in her head. She breathed deeply and risked a glance at Mrs Bailey. She, too, seemed to have forgotten the incident. Or had she? Bronia wished she knew.

Mrs Bailey put all the dishes in a pile on the draining-board. "Have you made your beds?" she asked.

Tommy nodded but William shrugged and said, "I will in a minute ..."

"You will now," said Mrs Bailey.

"Aw, Aunty Bee ..."

"Go on ..." she urged him and then looked at Bronia. "You, too, young lady. We all make our own beds here." The words hung in the air as if they were a challenge.

Bronia still could not bring herself to look at her. She just couldn't. It did not seem fair that she had told the total truth for once and it seemed that Mrs Bailey had not believed her. How was it, she wondered, that she could tell all sorts of stories and people would believe her? Then, when she told the truth for once, no one did! She sighed.

"All right," she mumbled, feeling a lump in her throat. "Come on, Ben, I'll make yours as well."

Her little brother scrambled down from the table and took hold of her hand. Bronia felt it – small, warm and trusting – and smiled down at him. Together they started slowly up the stairs, followed reluctantly by William and excitedly by Thomas.

Mrs Bailey watched them and then smiled

and said to herself, "She'll be all right, that one. She's learning ... God will show her the way."

"Will she get you, William?" asked Tommy as the door to the kitchen closed behind them. He pronounced his brother's name "Will-yum".

William shrugged. "I dunno," he said, and then added in a fit of bravado, "Probably!" His outward show of bravery, however, was ruined by his furtive glances up the stairs.

"What did you do?" asked Bronia.

"Same as always ..." grinned Tommy. "Sarah's scared of spiders! ..."

William smiled, looking at Bronia. "I put a big one on her pillow and sloshed a wet flannel in her face!" he beamed.

Tommy laughed delightedly and clapped his hands. Ben regarded both of them solemnly and stuck his finger in his mouth. He leaned on Bronia and she put a hand on his shoulder. She felt a small smile begin at the corner of her mouth.

"Why?" she asked.

"Sarah's naughty," repeated Tommy.

"Yes," agreed William. "She's always getting us into trouble. She does things and then makes out it's our fault. She takes biscuits and blames Tommy here." Tommy nodded vigorously.

"She doesn't like us much," he continued.

"Well, I'm not surprised if that's how you treat her!" exclaimed Bronia.

"No," William shook his head. "You don't understand. She doesn't like *anybody* much. . . . We wanted to be friends, but she kept going on about how her father was an airline pilot and a Harrods van was coming to bring her stuff. It was all lies, you know. You can tell, can't you, when someone is telling lies? . . ." He looked at Bronia with his shrewd knowing eyes.

"She's been here ages . . ." said Tommy, as if that explained everything.

Bronia looked at the two boys and suddenly felt that she understood a great deal more about Sarah than they did. She felt very sorry for her.

"Come on," said William. "We'd better get back to our room quickly before she comes out!" They both ran, laughing noisily, up the stairs.

When they had disappeared round the corner, Bronia was not sure that she could face going back into her own room until she had sorted out a few of her thoughts.

"We'll do your bed first," she said and led Ben along the corridor to his door. His room was very small, with just enough room for one single bed. It was the same height as all the other rooms though, and the window, which almost filled one wall, stretched nearly to the ceiling. More new wardrobes had been built in here and the walls were painted pale blue.

Ben's clothes had been put into a small, neatly-folded pile on the chair next to the bed.

WPC Jackson had obviously undressed him while he was still asleep last night, and put him into the green pyjamas he was wearing.

"You'd better put your clothes on," she said, pointing to the pile. He began to take his pyjama jacket off, taking great care to undo all the large buttons, while Bronia pulled the covers straight on his bed and smoothed them down. The middle still felt warm from where his tiny body had rested.

Ben triumphantly flung his jacket on the floor and wriggled and kicked until the pyjama bottoms came off. These he stood on while he grabbed his trousers, then he sat down on the floor to try to dress himself. He found it very difficult and struggled until Bronia had finished the bed and was able to help him.

"Can I go and play in the garden?" he asked when they had finished, looking through his window. This had a different view from Bronia's and as she stood next to him she saw the whole of the town spread out below them.

It was quite breathtaking. She tried to make out where they lived, but she was not sure even of the direction in which their home lay. For a moment she felt quite lost and empty.

Ben tugged at her skirt. "Can I, Mummy?" he asked, staring down at the lawn below them. "Can I play in the garden?"

Bronia realised with a jolt that he had called her "Mummy" and was still looking at the garden, unaware that he had made a mistake.

She knew then that for him she had for the moment taken the place of their mother.

"Aren't you going to help me make my bed?" she asked gently. "You haven't seen my room."

She knew that he would not be any help at all but she needed someone she knew to be with her, even if it was only her baby brother.

"OK," he agreed readily and slipped his hand into hers.

Bronia felt rather silly, but she listened at her door before pushing it open. There was no sound from inside so she thought that Sarah was either still asleep or in the bathroom.

"Come on," she whispered and tiptoed in. Sitting on Bronia's bed and wearing her brand-new blue cardigan was Sarah.

Bronia stopped. Ben clutched at her skirt and she put a hand on his head. He leaned against her and stuck his finger in his mouth.

"You've got my cardigan on," she said.

"So what?..."

"It's mine."

Sarah held her gaze for a moment, then sniffed and pulled it off. "It's a rubbishy cardigan anyway!" she sneered, throwing it on to the bed. She flicked a quick glance at Benjamin and looked away again.

"What did you have it on for, then?" asked Bronia, taking a step into the room with Ben shuffling along beside her, still leaning.

Sarah shrugged and got up. She folded her

arms. "I was cold. My things haven't arrived yet," she said grandly. "Daddy sent to Harrods for all the latest gear. It should be arriving any day now."

Bronia stared at her in her thin cotton nightdress. Sarah's fair curly hair was cut short and stray wisps of it stuck round her face and made it look like a cap. Sarah tossed her head suddenly as if she had made a decision. She began to make her bed expertly, throwing back the sheets and plumping up the pillows.

"I'm used to this," she said over her shoulder. "We always had to make our own beds at boarding-school in Switzerland."

"Oh." Bronia walked into the middle of the room. She did not know what to say. She began to make her bed slowly and thoughtfully. She had never met anyone before who shopped at Harrods or had been to boarding-school in Switzerland. Very faint warning bells rang in her mind but they were not quite loud enough for her to hear.

Ben ran over to the window. "It's more garden!" he called in an excited voice.

"Stupid kid!" snapped Sarah, straightening up. "I hate kids!"

"He's my brother," said Bronia. "He's only little."

"I'm not ... I'm big!" stated Ben, turning round.

"See – he's stupid!" hissed Sarah, giving a short laugh.

The two girls faced each other angrily in the middle of the room. One, whose long dark hair hung loosely about her shoulders, was fighting back the tears of frustration as she leapt to the defence of her baby brother. The other, taller, and with blonde bubbly curls, stood with her lips twisted in a sneer, looking haughtily down her nose.

"You've no right to say that!" spat Bronia, clenching her hands into hard fists.

"I have every right to say exactly what I like," said Sarah softly, defying anyone to disagree with her.

"He's my brother," repeated Bronia, doggedly.

"The poor thing!"

Bronia exploded. "Just because you've got a lot of money – or at least you say you have! – it doesn't mean that you can go around looking down on the rest of us!" she snarled.

As her rage gave vent to her feelings she did not think about what she was saying. The words just came tumbling out in a jumble.

"Just who do you think you are?" she demanded. "What makes you so great? You're no better than anyone else! . . . and don't pick on my little brother!" she ended with a shout.

Sarah stared at her. "You're pathetic!" she announced and flounced out of the room.

Bronia wanted to scream. She screwed her hands up tightly again and dug her nails into the palms. How dare that horrible girl look down on her! What made her so much better than anyone else?

"Bronia?" Ben pulled at his sister's skirt.

"What?"

"She's stupid, isn't she?" he said seriously, looking up at her. He did not quite understand what had happened, but he knew that his sister was upset and he did not like it.

Bronia relaxed a little and smiled, unshed tears shining in her eyes.

"Yes, she is," she said firmly. "Very."

8

More News

MRS COLE sat on the hard narrow bed in the hospitality room and pulled her tissue apart with trembling fingers. She looked at her watch. There was still half an hour to go before she could see the consultant about the results of the latest batch of tests.

John Cole had slowly regained consciousness as the morning wore on and had smiled at her, so she knew that he recognised her even though he had not spoken yet. She had sat there at his bedside holding his hand. Sometimes she felt sure that she could feel an answering pressure when she squeezed his fingers and she was glad.

The long morning dragged on but she could feel that he was gradually growing stronger. His breathing became deeper and more relaxed and once or twice he had slept properly. Although he had not said anything, she knew that he was comforted by her presence.

Later on, at about lunchtime, the nurse had ushered her out of the room while they examined him yet again. She had refused anything to eat, but the young nurse had brought her a cup of tea. It sat on the small white bedside table now, cold and untouched.

She shuddered as she remembered the doctor's awful words "... slight possibility that he may be paralysed ..." They kept coming back and ringing round and round her head. While she was in the room with her husband she refused to think about it. It was just too awful. But since she had been alone in this small bare room all her thoughts had focused on the dreadful possibility that her husband might be crippled.

She felt foolish now, remembering how she had fainted at the news, but the doctor had assured her that it was quite natural, especially after the uncomfortable night she had spent. She rubbed the bruise on the side of her head. She had gone down so suddenly that she had hit her head on the floor.

She looked at her watch again and stood up. It was nearly time to go. She combed her fingers through her dark hair and went in search of a nurse.

She walked nervously down the corridor and tapped gently on the door. It opened at her touch and as she stood there, she could see the doctor and nurse in deep conversation.

"Ah, Mrs Cole!" beamed the doctor as he looked up. "We were just discussing your husband," and he tapped the file on the table in front of him. It was now a great deal thicker than it had been that morning.

"Is he going to be all right?" she blurted out.

"Sit down, Mrs Cole," said the nurse, indicating the chair next to the desk.

"Is he all right?" she repeated, ignoring the seat.

"I'll not try to pretend that your husband has not been very seriously injured," began the doctor softly. "He's still very ill, but all the tests we've managed to do this afternoon show that there is every chance he will make a full recovery."

The nurse nodded and smiled as he spoke.

"Do you mean ...?" Bronia's mother could hardly believe it. They were actually telling her that her husband was going to be all right! She laughed out loud. "That's wonderful!" she cried, and felt hot tears spring suddenly into her eyes. She dabbed them away briskly with yet another tissue and sniffed loudly, wondering why she had spent half the night doubting that God existed. Here was all the proof she could ever have wanted.

"Now will you take a seat?" smiled the nurse. Marion Cole sat down this time, instantly, as if her legs had given way.

"It will take a long time," warned the doctor, but he, too, was smiling. "And he will probably be in a wheelchair for a while, but I can see no reason why he shouldn't get fully better and go back to work. He's a very lucky man."

"Oh, doctor! That's marvellous!" she grinned. "Can I go and see him?"

The doctor looked at the nurse, who nodded.

"I think so," he said. "But don't stay too long. He must have his rest if he's going to mend."

"Oh, thank you, thank you!" she said. They were all smiling now. All the dark clouds of gloom had been lifted.

"Should I ring Oak House for you?" asked the nurse. "After all, you won't need to stay here all the time now that you know he's on the mend, will you? Your children can come back home now, can't they?"

"Oh yes! Yes, of course!" exclaimed Mrs Cole. "I had completely forgotten about them. . . . I mean . . . I . . ." she stopped, horrified at what she had said, although it was perfectly true.

"I understand," said the nurse. "Your thoughts were fully occupied by your husband."

"Doesn't it sound awful?" said Mrs Cole. "I hadn't really forgotten them. . . . It's just . . . it's just that . . ."

"Don't worry about it," smiled the nurse, putting out a hand to pat her arm. "You just put them to the back of your mind for a while, that's all."

Mrs Cole nodded, trying to understand. "Is that wrong?" she asked seriously.

"Not at all," replied the nurse matter-of-factly. "As a wife and mother you must decide which things are most important at any one time. You knew that your children were in very good hands so you could give all your attention to your husband. And why not? He needed you far more last night than they did!"

"I suppose so," said Bronia's mother thoughtfully. She still could neither quite shake off the feeling of guilt, nor could she quite forgive herself.

The nurse opened the door and they went into the corridor. For a moment they walked side by side in silence; one briskly professional and the other deep in thought.

"You can tell Oak House that I'll collect them in time for tea," said Mrs Cole at last. "It's a good job it's Saturday and Bronia hasn't had to go to school."

"Right, I'll tell Mrs Bailey to expect you at about half past five, then. OK?"

"Yes, thank you. I must look a mess. I need to have a bath and wash my hair."

"You look fine ..." smiled the nurse, opening the door to the small intensive care unit. "Here we are, then, and remember, only a few minutes, now ..."

Marion Cole smiled and walked towards her husband.

9

Preparing for Home

BRONIA sat on the rug watching the flames as they flickered and danced. Ben was sprawled next to her, carefully drawing a picture with some crayons Mrs Bailey had found in her "treasure chest". The big kitchen certainly was the best room in the house.

Thomas and William had been collected by their father before lunch so that they could go to visit their mother together. Mrs Bailey had seen to it that they were both well scrubbed and tidy before she let them tear along the driveway to greet the tall man with the shock of red hair. Tommy leapt screaming into his father's arms and was swung round and round and high up into the air. William walked quickly until he could restrain himself no longer and broke into a trot so that his father could hug him too.

Mrs Bailey and Bronia watched them from the doorway.

"Their mother will be home soon," Mrs Bailey said, and Bronia noticed that she seemed a little sad. "They've promised to visit, though," she added, brightening. "All of them together when their mam's better."

Watching them, Bronia suddenly thought of her own father and wished and wished for him to be all right. This time she did not push the thoughts away but let them linger and multiply until they took over. She walked quickly back into the kitchen and sat down in front of the fire again.

She wished so hard that it almost hurt. She shut her eyes tightly so that she could not see the images of William and Tommy and their father any more. She now realised that she had deliberately not thought about her father because she dared not. She was frightened in case it was too late and he would never come home again. The thought terrified her. She twisted her fingers into the rug and stared into the fire.

Now, unbidden, the memories came flooding into her mind and she did nothing to stop them. She remembered how kind he always was and how he let Ben crawl all over him, even when he had come home tired from work. She thought of how he wrestled with both of them on the settee and how they all got into trouble with Mum, including Dad, and how he had giggled with them when she had gone out of the room again. He always had a funny story to tell them or sweets and comics for them. Ben said he had a "smiley face" and she knew just what he meant.

Suddenly she understood that it did not matter that he worked in a factory or that they lived in a small house and did not have a telephone. He was her and Ben's father who loved them and that was all that mattered. They were a family and nothing in the world could change that. They had something that made up for all the things they could not afford to buy. In fact, what they had could not be bought anyway. They were all loved and loved each other. She could see that now. She suddenly understood that when Ben had been born she had thought that her parents would love her less, but she could now see that it had not made any difference.

"If only," she whispered fiercely to herself. "If only Dad could get better and come home, then everything would be all right. Please, God, make him better."

She squeezed her eyes tightly shut again and swallowed hard. She dared not think that it might be too late. She would never forgive herself for looking down on him, especially if she did not have a chance to make it up to him – and her mother, of course.

Now, as she sat in front of the fire, she let her mind wander back to Sarah. What was it she had said? There would be a delivery van from Harrods? There had certainly been no sign of one so far that day. What about the Swiss boarding-school? . . . As she thought, Bronia remembered what William had said but she also found that there was something very familiar about the story Sarah had told her. At first she could not think what it was and then it suddenly dawned on her. When she had first arrived at Oak House – had it really only been last night? – she had made up a tale to tell about her father being a millionaire and her mother being a ballet dancer, as well as something about a Swiss boarding-school.

Could it be, she wondered, that Sarah lived in a fantasy world as she had done? Did she prefer to live in fairy tales instead of the real world? The thought was very odd. Bronia looked at the idea from all different angles and argued about it in her head but she always came back to the same conclusion.

The telephone rang in the hall and Mrs Bailey bustled out to answer it. Bronia got up and stretched. If she could persuade her mother and father, it would be great to have a coal fire at home.

"Well now, and that's wonderful," smiled Mrs Bailey, coming back into the room. "That was a nurse at the hospital and your mammy's coming to pick you up tonight." Bronia felt her heart turn over.

"Mummy's coming?" asked Ben, twisting round on the rug and chewing a crayon.

"Yes, my little love. Your mammy's coming to take you home."

"I'm drawing her a picture," he announced, turning back to his paper.

Bronia bit her lip. "How's Dad?" she asked rather timidly, afraid of the answer.

Mrs Bailey turned to her. "Well now," she

said, looking her straight in the face. "I thought you'd forgotten all about him."

"Oh . . . I . . ." began Bronia, shaken by the thought herself.

"I know," said Mrs Bailey kindly. "You daren't think about it?"

"How did you know?" Bronia stared at Mrs Bailey in wonder. Was there anything that this Irish woman did not understand?

"I know a lot more than you think," smiled Mrs Bailey, and Bronia nodded in agreement.

"How is Dad?" she repeated, more confidently this time.

"Well now, and that's the best news of all . . ." smiled Mrs Bailey. "He's going to be all right."

"Oh, that's wonderful!" cried Bronia. She flung her arms round the dumpy woman and hugged her, grinning broadly.

"Me too!" shouted Ben and ran up to cling to both of them.

"He'll be in hospital for a while yet, though," warned Mrs Bailey gently. "And then he'll be at home for a long time until he gets really better."

"That doesn't matter!" exclaimed Bronia. "He'll be at home with us! All together again!"

"Yes," said Mrs Bailey, looking down at her seriously. "But it does mean that your mammy is going to need an awful lot of help."

"That's all right," said Bronia, her cheeks flushed. "I'll help her."

Mrs Bailey's eyes twinkled. She smiled and said, "I'm sure you will," and then added under her breath, "... now."

Bronia looked up at her, straight in the eye this time. "Thank you," she whispered slowly.

"I knew you'd be all right," said Mrs Bailey. "Took a bit of a shock to sort you out, though."

"Yes," agreed Bronia, thoughtfully.

"I'm drawing a picture for Daddy," said Ben and he went back to his place in front of the fire.

"That'll be nice," said Mrs Bailey, returning to her baking.

Bronia hesitated. "Where's Sarah?" she asked.

"I expect she's up in her room," replied Mrs Bailey without looking up. "She stays up there quite a lot."

"Right," said Bronia. "I'll go and see her. I need to talk to her."

As the kitchen door clicked softly shut, Mrs Bailey looked up and smiled. "You'll do, lass," she whispered. "You'll do."

Bronia walked quickly up the stairs and down the corridor. She tapped gently on the bedroom door.

"Who is it?" came a voice.

"It's me."

"Oh." Sarah did not sound too pleased.

"Can I come in?"

"I suppose so, it's your bedroom too, isn't it?"

Bronia pushed open the door. Sarah was lying on her bed with a half-finished pencil drawing in front of her.

"Well?" she said.

"I want to talk to you," began Bronia, closing the door behind her.

"What about?"

"You ..."

"Pardon?"

"I want to talk to you."

"Why?"

Bronia could see that they were getting nowhere fast. She had to try a different approach. "Has the Harrods van been yet?" she asked airily.

"Are you taking the mickey?" began Sarah, putting down her pencil, a dark flush beginning on her cheeks which seemed to rub out all the freckles.

Bronia shook her head. She stood looking down at Sarah and then noticed the drawing. It was of a small boy. She looked closer. It was a perfect drawing of Ben!

"Hey! That's good!" she exclaimed.

Sarah flipped over the cover of her drawing-pad so that the picture was covered.

"Look," she said. "Just what is it that you want?"

Bronia sat down on the bed next to her.

"My father works in a factory ..." she began, taking a deep breath. Sarah made a tutting noise and raised her eyes to heaven.

". . . and my mother stays at home all day to look after Ben . . ."

"So what?" sneered Sarah, but Bronia ploughed on, ignoring her.

"My father's had a terrible accident at work and he's in hospital. My mother's with him now." She heard Sarah catch her breath but deliberately did not look at her.

She continued as if she were telling the story to herself for the first time. "Before I came here I thought we lived in a dump and I hated my little brother and despised my parents because they were so dull and ordinary."

Sarah stood up suddenly and went to stare out of the window with her back to the room. The drawing-pad flopped down to the floor and Bronia picked it up without thinking, smoothing the pages down before putting it back on the pillow.

She began again, finding the words easier now. "Since we've been here I have found out that I have an awful lot more than some people have. I don't mean things you can buy in a shop, I mean . . ." She stopped, not knowing how to express what she felt.

She started again, frowning in concentration. "I know that it seems like a good idea to tell lies about yourself to make you seem more interesting. I used to myself . . . but now I think that people either like you for yourself or not at all." She stopped, amazed at how her thoughts had come together so clearly at last.

She smiled suddenly. "And God loves you anyway, even though you don't seem to think much of yourself."

Bronia turned to Sarah. "So you see," she said "I *know* there's no Harrods van. I *know* there's no school in Switzerland. Huh! I even thought I'd try that one!" She shook her head now at the very thought.

She got up and walked round the bed towards the window.

"I *know*, Sarah. I *do know* ..." she said softly. "You don't need to make up all that stuff with me ... In fact, you don't need to do it for anybody!"

Beside her Sarah gave a stifled sob and Bronia could see the glistening wet tears on her cheeks. She put out her hand to touch the girl's arm. "Come on," she whispered. "It doesn't matter. It's not that important ... now. I'll not tell.... Come on, let's have another look at that drawing. I think it's great!"

She led the girl back to the bed again and they sat down next to each other, this time as friends.

Sarah sniffed loudly and wiped her eyes on the sleeve of her jumper. "I'm sorry," she said. "It's just that I know that no one can care for me ..."

Bronia knew instinctively that Sarah was not dramatising the situation. "Of course they can!" she said.

Sarah shook her head. "I've been here almost a year. Ever since my parents were killed in a car crash."

Bronia was horrified. She could not imagine anything more terrible. "Oh no ..." she said. "How awful ..." and felt very ashamed of ever having told a similar tale to gain sympathy. Now, faced with someone who had actually experienced it, it seemed too dreadful.

Sarah sniffed again and the words came out in a rush. "Everyone else here has somewhere to go after a few weeks. I'm the only one to be left behind.... Nobody wants me ..."

"There's Mrs Bailey ..."

"Yes, there's Aunty Bee," agreed Sarah with a wan little smile. "But she's not my own flesh and blood, is she? It's not the same."

"Isn't it?" asked Bronia. "She can't have children of her own so that is why she does this job. She loves kids ..."

"I know," nodded Sarah. "I do, too."

"But you said you hated them!" said Bronia, thinking of how horrible Sarah had been to Ben.

Sarah nodded again. "I know," she said. "That's because if I get too friendly with them and they go away, well ..." Her voice trailed off, and she shrugged.

"You didn't want to get hurt," finished Bronia.

Sarah nodded. "It doesn't ... *didn't* matter

what I told people. They didn't care.... They just stayed a couple of days and then went away again..."

Bronia looked at her and understood. "Well, my mum is coming for us this evening," she said, rather tactlessly.

"See! What did I tell you!" exclaimed Sarah and Bronia had to grab her to stop her from jumping to her feet.

"Wait a minute!" she cried, seeing the words as Sarah must have seen them. "What I meant to say was that you can come and meet her if you like.... Perhaps you would like to come and visit us ... come to tea or stay the night or something ..."

Sarah stared at her, her eyes shining wetly through the tears. "Do you mean it?" she asked incredulously. "Wouldn't they mind?"

"Of course they wouldn't," said Bronia smiling. "There's plenty of love to go round in our house!"